STARTING SCHOOL

WITH AN

ENEMY

STARTING SCHOOL
WITH AN

WITH AN

ENEMY

by Elisa Carbone

ALFRED A. KNOPF, NEW YORK

Library of Congress Cataloging-in-Publication Data
Carbone, Elisa Lynn.
Starting school with an enemy / by Elisa Carbone.
p. cm.
Summary: Worried about finding friends when she moves from Maine to
Maryland, ten-year-old Sarah gets off to a bad start by making an enemy of a boy.
ISBN 0-679-88639-7 (trade). — ISBN 0-679-98639-1 (lib. bdg.)
[1. Friendship—Fiction. 2. Moving, Household—Fiction.
3. Schools—Fiction.] I. Title.
PZ7.C1865St 1998
[Fic]—dc21 97-33366

Printed in the United States of America
10 9 8 7 6 5 4 3 2 1

For Daniel and Rachel,
with love

ONE

"I hate this thing." I took off my bike helmet and let it dangle like a dead fish.

Dad scratched his nose, but he didn't look up from his book.

"It's making my head sweaty. I'm going to go ride my bike without it." I dumped the helmet on the floor. "Maybe I'll get arrested."

Dad still didn't look up.

"Or maybe I'll get hit by a car."

He slapped his book shut. "You wore that helmet all the time in Portland. Why is it suddenly a problem?"

"Because it's *hot* here."

Most people go to Maine in the summer. My dumb family left Maine and moved to hot, sticky Maryland in August.

"There were hot days in Portland, too," my dad argued.

Why can't parents figure out when you're complaining about one thing but you're actually upset about another? "But they *make* you wear a helmet here. What if the wind blows real hard and knocks

1

my helmet off and just then a police car comes around the corner and there I am with no helmet? I'd have my first arrest at age ten. How am I supposed to get into college?"

Dad looked up at the ceiling, then at me. "They don't arrest you, honey. They give you a ticket. If you lost your helmet because of a wind gust, I'd pay the ticket. But if you—"

I'd already heard the "If You Forget to Wear Your Helmet, You'll Have to Pay the Fifteen-Dollar Ticket" speech, so I interrupted. "In Portland, I liked wearing my helmet because they didn't have a bunch of laws about it. I need freedom."

My dad raised one eyebrow at me. "This is about the move, not the helmet, right?"

Two points for Dad.

I nodded and stuck out my lower lip. He opened his arms so I could climb halfway onto his big belly and sniffle into his Boston Red Sox T-shirt. "Sarah, Sarah, Sarah." He patted me on the head and tried to sound reassuring. But somehow, hearing my name three times and being petted like a dog didn't make me feel any better. What I wanted him to say was "Hey! I almost forgot to tell you! Mom and I decided that we don't like it here in Maryland either and we're moving back to Portland this weekend, just in time for school to start."

2

Instead he just patted my head again. Sometimes I think he's still getting me mixed up with the dog. When I was a baby, we had a dog named Rasta, a cocker spaniel. Dad used to get our names mixed up for some reason. Rasta. Sarah. I guess both of us had curly blond hair and were getting around on all fours, but I still can't see confusing a kid with a dog.

At that moment my fifteen-year-old brother, Jerod, shoved open the front door, slammed it behind him, tromped over to the refrigerator, and pulled out a carton of orange juice. He spotted us on the couch, flopped down next to us, and said, "Wassup?"

Jerod needs a translator. He and his friends mostly grunt and mumble. He didn't even seem to mind moving. Three weeks in Maryland and he's already found a bunch of guys who go around saying things like "Watchupto?" and "Kive sum a dat?" It drives my mom crazy. Not my dad, though. My dad thinks kids need "freedom to express themselves." That's why he let Jerod pierce his ear and dye his hair black.

"Have you been playing basketball with the guys?" Dad asked.

"Eup." Jerod threw back his head and guzzled orange juice right from the container.

"So aren't you kids excited about starting school in a new state on Monday?"

Sometimes parents have really weird ideas about what is exciting in life.

"Nah," said Jerod.

I shook my head. School back home in Maine where I had my friends was okay. But in three weeks I hadn't met a single kid my age in the neighborhood, so I'd be starting school as a stranger.

"Think of it as an adventure!" said Dad.

He said the same thing before I went into the hospital to have my appendix out.

Jerod shrugged. "'Drather play basketball."

I decided to leave the two guys to talk and drink orange juice out of the carton. I figured I'd give my bike, and helmet, one more chance to be entertaining.

Outside it was muggy, the kind of hot that makes you feel itchy when you don't even have poison ivy. I stick to riding on the sidewalk because it's shadier and cooler there and because my mom told me if she ever catches me riding in the street she'll hang me upside down by my toes for three days. I think she was exaggerating, and anyhow, she was still away on one of her training trips for her new job, but I don't like to push my luck.

I was whipping down the sidewalk, head to the handlebars, wind filling up my T-shirt like a balloon, when I saw this kid. He had scrawny little pencil legs and was pedaling a red tricycle down a driveway toward the street.

I figured he'd stop when he got to the curb, but he just kept going. At that second I sucked in my breath because the other thing coming down the street was a huge pink Dy-Dee Diaper truck. It was headed right for the kid!

I don't know what I was thinking—maybe that I'd die a hero and not have to start fifth grade as a stranger after all—but I aimed my bike at the kid so I could cut him off before the truck hit him. I shouted and waved my arms. Maybe the kid was going faster than I thought, or maybe it was because I was riding with no hands, yelling, waving, and bumping over the curb all at the same time, but instead of cutting him off I rammed right into him.

The truck driver screeched on his brakes and veered to miss us. "You crazy brats! Get out of the street!" he bellowed out the window.

I would have yelled back that I'm not a crazy brat, that I was just saving the stupid kid on the tricycle, but the kid was screaming at the top of his lungs, so I just held my ears.

His knees were scratched up and bloody from where he'd landed on the pavement when I hit him, but I figured that was better than being squashed flat by a truck. I moved his trike onto the sidewalk. "You've got to get out of the street," I said real loud so he could hear me over his screaming. He didn't budge.

A red-haired boy burst out of the house, stomped down the driveway, and scooped the screaming kid into his arms.

"She—she hit me," the little brat whimpered. Then he started blubbering all over again.

"He was about to get squashed by the Dy-Dee Diaper truck," I explained.

The big kid's eyes got real small in the middle of his freckled face. "You must be a real sicko to pick on tiny little kids."

"I didn't hit him on purpose!"

"Oh, yes, you did. I saw the whole thing." He sneered at me.

"If you saw the whole thing, then you must have seen the *truck!*" I cried. I couldn't believe he was being so dense.

His neck turned red and the color crept up to his cheeks.

"You were 'posed to be watching me, Eric," his little brother informed him between dry sobs.

Eric glared at me like I was some kind of disgusting fungus creature. Then he whisked the brat up the driveway to the house. Just before the screen door shut I heard him say, "When Ma gets home, we're going to tell her how that nasty girl hurt you."

I must have stood there for a full five minutes waiting for someone to say, "Cut. Cut. That was terrible. Let's do the scene again, and this time everybody jump up and down and praise Sarah for saving the little boy's life."

But nobody did. A lady walking her dog said, "Is that your bike in the road? You'd better get it out of there."

As I rode home, I kept thinking how Eric looked pretty close to my age. And the only thing worse than starting school as a stranger is starting school with an enemy.

TWO

"Sarah, are you up?"

It was early on Sunday morning and I was in bed with my eyes closed and probably my mouth open, snoring, before Dad jiggled my arm.

"Sarah, can I borrow one of your hair elastics?"

That's how I knew it was another hot day. My dad doesn't have much hair on top of his head, so he makes up for it by growing it long in back. When it's hot, he uses my elastics to put it in a ponytail.

"Sure," I mumbled.

"Thanks. Are you ready for some breakfast?"

I peeked at the clock. I'd been sleeping until after ten all summer, and here he was waking me up at seven thirty A.M. on Sunday to ask me if I wanted to eat. I knew what he was doing, though. He was trying to get me "on schedule" because school would be starting the next day. I'd rather stay off schedule one more day.

"Nope," I said, and pulled the covers over my head.

"I made pancakes," he said in a singsong voice like he was doing a commercial.

"No thanks." I shut my eyes tight, but I was becoming more and more awake. I had this awful feeling I was getting on schedule after all.

Dad opened the blinds and went over to my poster box. "Maybe you can hang some of these today," he said.

I didn't mean to groan in such an obnoxious way. It just came out. I'd left that box packed because I had this feeling that if I didn't put any pictures on the walls, then maybe I wouldn't have to stay. Dad left me alone to be grumpy.

I dragged myself out of bed and put on a pair of cutoffs and a baggy T-shirt. Then I dumped the contents of my poster box onto the floor. I had a poster of Michael Jordan about to make a slam dunk, a green and white Boston Celtics banner, a Save the Seals poster with a sad, fluffy baby seal on it, a blown-up picture of me when I was seven playing Tinker Bell in *Peter Pan* for the school play, and about a million snapshots of me and Andrea, my best friend from back in Portland. I pouted. Three weeks and Andrea hadn't even written to me. I hadn't written to her either, but why should I if she wasn't writing to me?

That was one of the weirdest things about moving: not living across the street from Andrea anymore. We'd lived on that street forever, and she was just always *there*. We started out as babies, probably drooling on each other and hitting each other over the head with rattles. Then we moved on to tea parties, then dog-chasing (she got a puppy when we were both seven), and finally sleepovers, especially on Friday nights before Saturday-morning softball practice. In fact, we spent the night at each other's houses so often, our parents could lose track of where we were. One Saturday my dad took Jerod to his baseball practice and left me and Andrea upstairs sleeping. He thought we were at Andrea's house and her parents were taking us. Our coach didn't think that was a good excuse for missing practice, though.

Now we live across the street from four college guys with car alarms that go off in the middle of the night. I gave the posters a little shove with my foot, left them on the floor, and wandered downstairs to eat cold pancakes. Jerod was slumped at the kitchen table drinking coffee with his eyes closed. Dad must have been getting him on schedule, too.

Halfway through my pancakes there was a knock at the door. Jerod went to answer it because his friends were the only people who knew or cared where we lived these days. A minute later he came back into the kitchen, looked right at me, and said, "Sumbuy's ear tuh seya."

Then he sat down, closed his eyes, and stuck his nose back into his coffee mug.

Jerod mumbles worse when he's sleepy, so it took me a second to translate. "Somebody is here to see *me?*" I asked.

He nodded.

Probably somebody selling something and Jerod is too sleepy to get rid of them, I thought. I marched down the front hallway and peeked out the screen door. There was a girl with sparkly dark eyes humming to herself. When she saw me, she grinned. I was just about to say "Sorry, we don't want any," when she said, "Hi, I'm Christina Perez and we've been gone mostly all summer in El Salvador, but we got back last night and this morning we got our mail from our neighbor Mr. Hawkins and he said he saw a girl my age move into this house so I came over to see what grade you're in."

I opened the screen door and stepped outside. "Fifth," I said.

Christina's eyes lit up even more. "Me too! This is so great—it's the first time there's been somebody my age on this street. A girl, I mean. Who will your teacher be?"

"Mr. Harrison," I answered.

Christina pumped her fist. "Yes! Mine too."

"Cool," I said, grinning. "Where's your house?"

She pointed at the houses down the street, but over them, like she was trying to throw something.

"Down there. It's not far."

Listening to her talk, I tried to figure out what sounded funny. Then it hit me. She didn't have a Maryland accent. She had a Spanish accent. "Are you from El Salvador?" I asked.

She threw her hands over her mouth and giggled. "I've been speaking Spanish all summer and my tongue is mixed up!"

"I like your accent. It sounds neat." I hoped I hadn't insulted her during our first ninety seconds together.

"It'll be gone in two weeks—you'll see." She waved her hand like she was shooing away gnats.

I didn't get it. How could somebody lose a foreign accent so fast? But I decided not to ask any more questions because so far I really liked her and I didn't want to say anything too stupid. "My name's Sarah. You want to come in?" I asked, and opened the door.

Christina shook her head. "I can't come into your house until my parents meet your parents. But you can come to my house. You want to?"

I wasn't sure if this was a Maryland thing or an El Salvador thing, where you can have someone over, but you can't go to their house. "Sure," I said. "I'll go tell my dad."

When I told my dad, I tried not to sound too enthusiastic. I didn't want him to think that one friend made everything about the move okay, but actually I was feeling pretty excited. Meeting Christina meant that I'd have someone to ride my bike with and someone to hang out with after school. And it meant that I wouldn't be starting school as a stranger.

Dad was in the living room reading the Sunday paper.

"There's this girl here and I'm going to her house, okay?" I said. I shrugged so he wouldn't think it was any big deal.

He looked at me as if I'd just announced we'd won the Maine lottery. "Oh, honey, that's terrific! See, I told you you'd make friends soon. Didn't I tell you that? What's her name? Does she live nearby? Come here and give me a big hug!"

I hate it when parents overreact. I told him her name and that she lived down the street and squirmed out of the hug before Christina decided she was tired of waiting for me.

Our street is pretty long, and the houses all look a lot alike, but the moment I saw Christina's house I knew I'd never have a problem finding it. The front yard had rounded flower beds with red, white, and yellow chrysanthemums and perfectly shaped bushes. Their front walk was so clean it looked like someone had scrubbed it with a toothbrush.

Christina's mother greeted us at the door with a mop in her hand. "Hello, hello. You stay outside—the floor is wet. In a little while you come in the kitchen and I make you a snack." She talked fast and cheerfully just like Christina, only with much more of a Spanish accent. Christina introduced us and then said she had just gotten a new soccer ball and would I like to try it? I grinned really wide when she said that. I'd always wished I could find a friend—a girl—who liked sports as much as I do. Andrea only went to softball because I did and because her parents wanted her to do something other than watch cartoons and eat Cocoa Puffs on Saturday mornings. And last year she was starting to get into really boring stuff like wanting to French-braid my hair and try on her mother's makeup. Once I let her paint my fingernails silver, but I felt like they couldn't breathe, so I made her take it off before my fingers suffocated. So the fact that Christina was the one suggesting we go outside and kick a ball around made me really happy.

There were empty flowerpots on the porch, and we put them in the grass to mark our soccer goals at either end of the yard.

"You can have the ball first," said Christina. She threw it to me.

"I'm going to score, I hope you know," I said. I hadn't played much soccer, but I was always one of the best players on my softball team and Jerod says I'm better at basketball than any girl he's ever seen, so I figured I could start bragging right from the start.

"Oh, really!" said Christina, smiling.

I kicked it in from my end and drove toward her goal. Christina met me in the middle, swiped the ball, and started toward my goal. I tried to steal the ball back, but she was dribbling so fast I couldn't get a foot in edgewise. At the end of the yard she gave the ball a smashing kick and it shot between my flowerpots.

"One nothing, my favor," she said.

I sighed. "Okay, you start this time." I decided maybe it would be easier to get the ball away from her if I could meet her head-on rather than having to chase her. It wasn't. She dribbled right past me and scored again.

"Two nothing," she said. "You want me to throw it in to you this time so you can block it in the air?"

"Sure," I said. Any new strategy sounded worth a try.

She stood out-of-bounds and threw the ball over her head. I meant to block it with my chest, but at the last second I saw it was higher than that, so I ducked and bounced it off my head. My teeth jammed shut on my tongue.

I groaned and held my mouth. I could taste blood.

Christina caught the ball and gave me a very worried look. "You're supposed to keep your teeth together when you do that," she said.

"I didn't know I was going to do that," I said. I touched my tongue to see if it was still bleeding.

Christina came close and told me to stick out my tongue. She looked cross-eyed as she examined it. "It's not too bad," she said. "You want me to teach you how to head the ball right? My cousins in El Salvador taught me this summer."

My mom used to tell me not to hit the ball with my head because it might cause brain damage, but Christina said all the kids in El Salvador know how to do it, and their brains are just fine, so I let her teach me. She showed me how to use the top part of my forehead so it wouldn't hurt so much, and how to throw my body back and then snap it forward to make the ball fly. And she helped me remember to clench my teeth right as the ball was coming at me. It was a lot of fun. We did passes, shots, and traps with our heads until both of us had headaches and felt like we were going to throw up. I was glad when Mrs. Perez called us inside.

Christina and I washed our hands and faces in the bathroom. Then we sat at the kitchen table and Mrs.

Perez asked me questions about Maine and my family and what I liked in school. As we talked, she pulled avocados, lemons, and tortillas out of the fridge.

"Your mother, she works?" Mrs. Perez asked. Her black hair was pulled straight back, but some of the curls had gotten loose and she blew them off her face as she worked.

"Yeah," I said. "My dad too."

"Good. Good," said Mrs. Perez. She was moving so fast my eyes could hardly keep up with her. She threw the tortillas into a skillet to sizzle, then sliced an avocado in half and mashed each half right in the shell. She chopped up the lemon with a scary-looking cleaver and squeezed some of the juice into the avocado mush. She added a pinch of salt and handed me and Christina an avocado half each. Then she threw the hot, crispy tortillas on a paper towel in front of us on the table.

"This is good. You will like it," she said.

Christina and I broke the tortilla into pieces and used it to scoop up the avocado-lemon-salt mixture. It was terrific.

"Wow," I said. "What do you call this stuff?"

Christina giggled. "Haven't you ever had guacamole?"

I stared at the green mush and the chunks of tortilla. I felt pretty stupid. "Well, yeah," I said, "but my mom buys it from the freezer section and she gets the tortilla chips from a plastic bag."

Christina didn't act like she thought I was stupid. She just smiled, scooped up another glob of guacamole, and stuffed it into her mouth.

When we were finished eating and I'd thanked Mrs. Perez about twenty times, Christina invited me up to her room to meet her hamster, Tito. It was the cleanest kid's room I've ever seen. Tito's cage didn't even stink. She let me hold him, and he crawled up my arm to my shoulder and sniffed my ear. Basically, I was feeling like I'd just found the nicest friend in the world and that maybe school wouldn't be too bad after all. I walked around her room to look at the stuff she had on the walls. She had a poster of a bunch of soccer players with D.C. UNITED printed across the top, a surfing poster, and next to that a picture of herself with her arm around a girl with curly black hair and olive skin. They were both smiling great big smiles.

"Who's that?" I asked.

"That's Rosa," said Christina. "She's my best friend."

I felt my stomach sink down to my knees. One minute I thought I'd met this great friend and school was going to be okay, and the next minute I found out I was just her neighborhood friend and her really best friend would probably be doing everything with her in school. I put Tito back into his cage.

"I've got to go help my dad with—uh, something," I said. I figured whatever my dad was doing, I'd go help him with it just so I could get out of there fast.

Christina didn't seem to notice what a bad mood I'd gotten into. She walked me to the door and said she'd see me tomorrow in school. I must be allergic to hamsters because I sniffled the whole way home.

THREE

Monday morning I got up extra early for two reasons. One, it was the first day of school, and two, my mother was finally home from her training classes (I knew because she'd kissed me in the middle of the night), and I needed time to convince her that I shouldn't go to school.

Dad and Jerod had already left for the day, and Mom was sound asleep on her back with her toes pointing at the ceiling. Mom is short and thin. She says I'll probably be taller than she is in a couple of years because I'm more big-boned like Dad.

I stared at her to wake her up. That's the basic difference between moms and dads. Dads you have to throw cold water on to wake up, but with moms all you have to do is look at them.

She opened one eye. "Mornin', sweetie." She held out her arm for a hug. "You getting ready for school?"

"Yeah." That was the truth. I was getting ready to

get out of going to school. "Are you going to work today?"

She nodded, both eyes closed again. Her new government job is the whole reason we came to Maryland in the first place. She was all excited about it, and my dad figured he could find carpentry work anywhere, so we moved.

I decided to get right to the point. "Except I can't go to school."

"Oh?" She opened both eyes this time.

"I don't have any friends."

"Dad said you spent the morning yesterday with a girl from your class. How is that not having any friends?"

"Christina already has a friend."

Mom frowned. "Nobody's allowed to have more than one friend around here?"

"That's not all." I climbed onto the bed with her. "You know how dangerous schools are these days. I heard half the kids in my class carry guns."

She sat up and looked at me seriously. "So you're really nervous about starting school in a new place, huh?"

Nothing gets past my mom. The line about the guns might have worked on my dad, but not her.

"You probably wish you were back home with Andrea and all your old friends, right?" she continued.

She ran her hands through her short hair. It stuck straight up on one side of her head and was mashed down on the other, like she'd gotten it caught in the blender before she went to bed.

"Yeah, but there's this guy who probably wants to beat me up. It's *violent* around here."

She folded her legs cross-legged and sighed. "Okay, why does this guy want to beat you up?"

"He thinks I ran over his little brother with my bike."

"But you didn't, right?"

"I did, but for a very good reason, and he doesn't seem to understand that."

Mom gave me a stern look. "You found a very good reason to run over a little kid?"

I didn't want to go into too much detail here because I had ridden in the street to save the kid. "I was protecting him from a truck," I said quickly. "Anyhow, now the guy hates me, so I need to stay home where it's safe."

Mom shook her head. "Sarah, please get dressed for school. If you're really worried about your safety, I'll drive you there and walk you to your classroom."

Mom can be understanding for just so long. I told her no thanks about the ride to school, though. I didn't want to look like a total dork. Dad said on the first day my teacher would be on the playground holding a sign that said MR. HARRISON, like those people in airports who are meeting strangers. Then Mr. Harrison would take me and the other kids to our classroom. I could have gone in on kindergarten roundup day to see my room since I was a new student, but I didn't see any reason to act like a kindergartner.

Back in my bedroom I examined the decorating job I'd done the night before. Snapshots of me and Andrea covered the wall above my dresser. There was the one of us standing on the rocks at Pemaquid Point, another of us hiking on Mt. Katahdin, and one of us dressed up like punk rockers for Halloween. Then there were a bunch of those strips from the photo booth at the Maine Mall with us making goofy faces. I wished I had one of us with our arms around each other like in Christina's picture of her and Rosa, but Andrea and I didn't do that kind of thing very much.

I pulled on my clothes and brushed my hair into a ponytail. I heard Mom downstairs in the kitchen clanging things around like she was thinking about cooking breakfast.

"Sarah, do you want eggs?" she called up the steps.

"Sure," I said. Eating breakfast with her would

give me one more chance to bug her about not going to school.

While I was busy slicing the white part off my fried eggs so I could put the yellow part on my toast, I decided to give it another try. "I hear home schooling is really big around here," I said.

Mom looked at me straight. "Sarah, your father and I both work. Who is going to home-school you?"

That's just like my mom. She always skips the in-between discussions like, "Oh, really? What makes you bring up the topic of home schooling, dear?" and gets right to the point.

"Are you sure you don't want me to walk you to your classroom?" she asked, sounding nicer.

I shook my head.

I suppose one good thing about Maryland is that our house is close to school and I get to walk. That way I can't miss the bus anymore. The only problem is, I can be late. And by the time I'd procrastinated by eating my eggs as slowly as possible, brushing my teeth, flossing them, and then brushing them again with a different flavor of toothpaste, I was pretty late.

There were no groups of kids on the playground when I got there, and no teachers holding friendly signs. I could tell it was going to be very interesting trying to find my classroom.

I was hurrying across the playing field when I

heard someone yell, "Hey, bozo! Don't walk too fast—you're gonna fall and smash your face."

I looked around. Three boys were sitting on the bars of the jungle gym. All three of them were looking at me. The one in the middle was Eric.

I stopped. "Let me guess," I said. "You have no life, so you sit on that stupid jungle gym all day and yell things at people."

Eric swung his legs back and forth. "It's just that we wouldn't want you to hurt yourself," he said in a sticky-sweet voice. "We know how uncoordinated you are!" They all laughed and hooted like hyenas.

I couldn't think of a good comeback for that one, so I just yelled, "I am not uncoordinated!"

They jumped down from the bars and ran past me. "You're late, bozo," Eric shouted over his shoulder as the last bell rang.

I hate being late. I especially hate being new and late. I ran to the school doors, then walked in trying to look like I knew what I was doing. I decided to try the peek-and-slip method of classroom finding. That's where you don't go to the office and admit you're both late and lost but instead walk down the halls and peek into all the classrooms until you see someone you recognize and then slip in quietly. All I had to do was find Christina.

The first four classrooms had little kids in them, so I kept on walking. The next one had big kids but a lady teacher. When I looked into the next one, I froze. There were kids about my age, and in the back of the room Eric was standing at the pencil sharpener. My heart started pounding real fast, but before I could keel over, I saw the blackboard. It said WELCOME TO THE SIXTH GRADE. I hurried down the hall.

I was really relieved when I finally found Christina. I figured the tall guy in the front of the room must be Mr. Harrison. Everyone was already sitting at desks arranged in groups of four facing one another. Mr. Harrison was talking.

"Ah, you must be Sarah," he said when I stepped through the door. His voice was deep and strong. He held out his hand for a handshake. I liked being treated like an adult that way, and our hands looked nice together: mine the color of oatmeal cookies and his the color of dark chocolate.

Christina jumped up and grabbed my arm. "Mr. Harrison put you in my work group," she said. She pulled me over to a desk, and I sat down facing a girl with thick eyebrows and red fingernails named Kelly, a kid with short, stubby dreadlocks named Jamal, and Christina. I knew their names because they were stuck to their desks on strips of paper like those nametags first graders have to wear on field trips. My name was on my desk, too. I glanced around the room, but I didn't see Christina's best friend Rosa anywhere.

"These are your cooperative learning groups," Mr. Harrison was saying. "You will work on projects together, and when your group does exceptionally well in completing an assignment, all four members will have their names posted on the Super Achievers board." He showed us a poster that had blue and silver stars like fireworks all over it.

Christina passed me a note. "Let's eat lunch together, okay?"

I nodded, but I didn't send a note back. No sense getting in trouble on my first day of school.

We spent the morning going over safety rules, meeting the librarian, touring the media center, and making sure everyone knew whose cubby was whose so nobody would end up with the wrong boots or sandwich or anything.

At lunchtime I was glad to have Christina to guide me around. The cafeteria was much bigger than the one in my school in Portland, and I wouldn't have known that the fifth graders sat at the tables closest to the doors, that the milk line was different from the food line, or that when the lights got turned off it meant we were being too noisy and we had to stop talking. It was also nice to have Christina to duck behind when we went to buy milk. We had to walk right by Eric's class, which was sitting at the tables farthest from the doors.

I kept searching the girls' tables from the other fifth grade—that's the way we all sat, girls together and boys together—but I still couldn't find Rosa. Finally, halfway through my cheese sandwich, I couldn't stand wondering anymore. "Is Rosa sick today or something?" I asked Christina.

She made a face at me. "How should I know?"

"Is she in another class or what? Does she go to another school?"

Christina laughed right into her milk. "Of course she goes to another school! Rosa lives in El Salvador."

I smiled so big, lettuce and sprouts stuck out of my mouth. But I didn't say, "That's great! I'm really glad she doesn't live around here." I figured that would be rude.

Christina told me to hurry and eat because kids would be choosing sides for a soccer game during recess and she didn't want to miss getting on a team. I gobbled my sandwich.

The second we walked outside I heard, "Uh-oh. Look out, she might run into you. It's the wacko girl!"

I wanted to punch Eric right in the stomach and watch him lose his lunch.

I tried to walk quickly past, but Eric followed us to where Jamal and another kid, Tyrone, were picking teams for soccer.

"We get Christina," Jamal called.

"I wouldn't pick her friend if I were you," said Eric. "She can't even ride a bike straight without falling all over the place." He stumbled around to demonstrate. "She'd probably kick the ball into the other team's goal."

"I would not!" I shrieked. "Your little brother is the uncoordinated one. I wouldn't have hit him if he wasn't about to get killed!"

"See what I mean?" Eric said calmly to the team captains. "She plays with my five-year-old brother and can't even get along." Then he walked away shaking his head.

I would have run after him and pounded him good, but I didn't want to miss the soccer game. So I stood around trying to look relaxed and coordinated, waiting for the teams to get picked.

All of a sudden I heard, "Let's go!" Two teams of kids ran toward the soccer field, Christina with them, and left me standing there.

That's when I decided I was going to make Eric sorry.

FOUR

"Not everyone gets picked every day." Christina tried to cheer me up.

"At this rate I won't get picked *ever*," I whined. It was already Thursday and I hadn't gotten to play soccer yet.

But I had an idea. All I needed to do was prove to Jamal and the other kids that I wasn't a total dingbat on the soccer field or anywhere else.

Our classroom had a closet with shelves of scissors and construction paper, extra textbooks, Mr. Harrison's real talking drum from Nigeria, and a huge bin filled with stuff for indoor recess like soft kidney-bean-colored rubber balls, jump ropes, and one very new-looking Spalding basketball. It was the basketball I'd noticed when Mr. Harrison sent me to the closet for scissors.

Some parents teach their kids to read when they're three years old or teach them to swim when they're two. My dad taught me how to play basketball when I was four. I guess it was mostly because he and Jerod were always playing out in the driveway, and Mom would say, "Go see what Daddy's doing," so I'd leave her alone. I was kind of forced into it. My dad figured if I was old enough to walk, I was old enough to dribble a basketball, and by the time I was six I could do lay-ups.

The new Spalding in the box definitely got my attention. So did Mr. Harrison when he told us how last year's fifth graders wrecked a bunch of the sporting equipment. He'd bought new stuff with his own money, but it was only for rainy days because we had jungle gyms and trees and Tyrone's old soccer ball to play with outside. "The supply closet is a place you go with permission ONLY. Is that understood?" he'd said like he meant it. And we all nodded our heads like marionettes.

But there was a hoop on the playground.

During lunch I could hardly swallow my food. I really liked Mr. Harrison, and I didn't want to make him mad. Still, I couldn't stand the thought of moping around on the playground for the rest of the year while Christina played soccer. My plan was to borrow the basketball for long enough to show what I could do with it, then return it unharmed before Mr. Harrison noticed.

"Are you ready for recess?" Christina asked. She bunched her lunch trash into a wad.

"Uh—I'll meet you outside. I've got to go to the classroom for a second," I said.

Christina shook her head. "You're not allowed."

"But I have to!" It was true. I was desperate.

"What for?" Christina asked.

I thought fast. Probably too fast. "I—I've got my period," I blurted out.

Christina's eyes got big and her mouth dropped open. I got out of there before she could ask me any questions. I'm sure I'll have to wait until I'm at least nineteen before I actually get my period, but it was the only thing I could think of to say.

In the hall I passed a whole line of first graders. I smiled at their teacher, and she didn't ask me for a hall pass.

Our classroom looked weird with no kids in it. It was so quiet I could hear my heart pounding in my ears like I was under water.

I yanked open the supply closet door, grabbed the Spalding, and hurried down the hall and out the back doors to the playground.

Eric was perched on a metal railing like an orange-headed rooster. "Look at that. The wacko girl thinks she can play basketball."

I walked right by without even looking at him. On the blacktop under the hoop I dribbled the ball a few times. It was a little low on air, but not bad.

I went into action. I did a lay-up from the right, dribbled out to the line, swished a foul shot, did a running one-hander along the baseline, and finished the show with a jump shot from the left. Four baskets in a row.

"You going to call me uncoordinated *now*, you creep?" I spun the ball on one finger and glared at Eric.

"I get Christina and Sarah on my team," I heard Jamal call, and I was sure Eric wasn't the only one who had seen my four baskets in a row.

Not the only one by a long shot. A tall shadow fell on the blacktop next to me. I turned slowly and found myself looking into Mr. Harrison's scowling face. Without a word he pointed to the doors. Eric started snickering, but Mr. Harrison gave him a look that shut him up.

I hung my head and started toward the doors. If Mr. Harrison was one of those mean teachers who uses any excuse to yell at you, I wouldn't have felt so bad. We passed Christina on her way out to recess. One glance at her told me she knew I'd lied about why I was going to the classroom.

As soon as we got inside, Mr. Harrison started bawling me out. "Sarah, I *know* you heard me yesterday when I gave that long explanation about the supply closet." And he went on about how he never would have expected me to be a student he'd have to keep his eye on, and he was disappointed in me for disobeying the rules, and I'd better shape up or it was going to be a very long year because he was not a teacher to be messed with. It made me feel much better. I always really appreciate it when adults yell at me when I'm in a lot of trouble. That way I know exactly where I stand.

He marched me to the classroom to pick up my books, then dropped me off at recess detention. He said I'd be spending today and all of next week there. The teacher sitting at the desk *did* look like the kind of mean teacher who uses any excuse to yell at you, so I made sure to sit very still and do my homework without even looking up.

That afternoon we divided into groups to go to art and dance, and Christina wasn't in my group. I didn't get to talk to her, but I could tell by the way she wouldn't look at me that she was angry. Sometimes you can tell just by looking at the back of someone's head that they're so mad at you they could spit.

When school let out, I trotted after her on her way walking home. "Christina, slow down. I need to tell you something."

She spun around to face me. "What? More lies?"

We just stood there looking at each other. I was

trying to think of what you're supposed to say when you have a brand-new friend and you do something really stupid and you think you might be about to lose their friendship.

"No more lies," I said.

She looked less angry.

We walked together toward home and I told her the whole story about Eric's little brother and the bikes and how Eric just seemed to want to be mad at me.

"That Eric, he's a pain in the you-know-what," she said, and threw her hand up like we both should just give in to the truth of it. "He picked on me last year for a while. He called me a wetback, which means he thinks my family and I *swam* here from El Salvador instead of coming into the country legally, which is totally ridiculous because my parents became citizens a long time ago and so did my brother, and I was born here so I'm just an American, and anyhow I'm not even a very good swimmer."

"That's mean," I said. "What did you do?"

She shrugged. "Nothing. My father told me people like that aren't even worth getting mad at and told me to ignore him. I acted like he wasn't there and he stopped teasing me after a while."

"I can ignore Eric," I said. "But I had to take the basketball. Otherwise I'd never get picked for soccer."

"But I wasn't going to let them keep leaving you out!" Christina exclaimed. "I was going to teach you some more stuff this weekend and then tell them to give you a try on Monday."

"Really?" I asked. I could understand why she wouldn't want to skip the soccer game just because I wasn't playing. If it had been basketball, I would have done the same thing. So I'd assumed she was just going to keep leaving me on my own for recess.

"Really," she answered. Then she gave me an annoyed look. "But now you can't play all next week because of detention."

I grimaced. "Oh, yeah." I fiddled with the strap of my backpack. "But I'll get picked the week after for sure, and I'll be really nice to Mr. Harrison from now on. I'll follow the rules and he'll forget all about it."

We walked a little ways without talking. Then Christina said, "You don't really get your period at all yet, right?"

"Right," I admitted.

"I thought so." She narrowed her eyes.

"I don't shave my legs yet either," I offered.

"Yeah, me neither. How about deodorant?"

"Nope," I said.

Christina was quiet. "Have you ever kissed a boy?"

"No! Yuck!"

We both started giggling. I walked her home and by the time we got to her house, we were friends again.

FIVE

"He was probably calling the parents of all the fifth graders to welcome them to school. I seriously don't think you need to call him back."

Just my luck. Mr. Harrison had phoned and Jerod actually remembered to take a message for my mom.

"It doesn't sound like a welcome call, Sarah. If I'm reading Jerod's handwriting correctly, it says, 'Would like to discuss Sarah's behavior with you.'"

"Jerod's handwriting? Ha-ha. Let me see."

She handed me the phone message and crossed her arms over her chest. I knew I was sinking fast.

"Behavior? That's not 'behavior,' that's 'bee-hive.' We're doing a science project with insects and he probably needs to know if I'm allergic to bees or honey or anything. I can tell him for you tomorrow."

By now my mom was rubbing her forehead like I'd given her a headache. "I'll call him and find out," she said.

My stomach kind of flipped over. I didn't want to listen to them planning my punishment, so I went outside to shoot hoops in the driveway. Jerod heard me and came out to play Horse.

"Bank shot," he said. Sometimes Jerod forgets he's a teenager and talks just like a normal person. "Why'd your teacher call?"

I made a face.

"You in trouble already?" he asked. He made the shot and handed me the ball.

"It's no big deal," I said. I missed and got an H. "I'll be done with detention soon, and then I'll stay out of trouble for the rest of the year."

"Cool," said Jerod. "From the line." He shot and missed, and it was my turn.

"Backward, no looking." That shot drives Jerod crazy. For some reason I can stand with my back to the basket, throw the ball over my head, and get it in about half the time. I turned, shot, and heard the ball swish through the basket.

"Geez, Sarah, how do you do that?" Jerod positioned himself, peeked upside down at the basket, and shot. The ball flew onto the roof, bounced once on the rain gutter, and landed in Mom's pansies. It did that just as Mom walked out the door.

"Sarah Marie, get that basketball out of my flower garden and get yourself into this house!" she screeched.

Jerod grabbed the ball and gave me a look like, "Whoa! Mom's not usually *this* mad."

Inside, I got two lectures: one on "Respect for Other People's Property" and the other on "Doing What the Teacher Tells You." I actually agreed with everything she said. Somehow I just end up doing the opposite sometimes.

I promised my mom I'd shape up. She decided the recess detention was enough punishment and I didn't get grounded or anything. I just had to weed and water all the pansies that hadn't gotten smashed by the basketball.

That night Christina called. "My parents said I can invite you to come to the beach with my father and me this weekend because Antonio, my big brother, has to work, so he can't go and my mother is staying home to make sure Antonio doesn't starve to death, so my father says there is plenty of room and we'll be leaving at eight thirty on Saturday morning. Can you come?" she asked.

I told her to hold on a minute. In Portland the beach was about fifteen minutes from our house, and Saturday was the day we usually went, so it was nice to think of doing something just like back home.

"Christina invited me to go swimming with her on Saturday. Can I go?" I asked.

Mom and Dad were in the living room and they had been reading, but when I asked them the question, they started looking at each other and rolling their eyes and making faces. That was because they really wanted to let me go because they wanted me to have a good time and be happy about living in Maryland, so they wanted to say yes. But they also didn't want to seem too nice right after I'd done such a bad thing in school, so they thought maybe they should say no. They didn't know what to say, so they just made faces instead. I decided a little begging might put them over the edge.

"Please?" I whined.

"Oh, all right," said my mother.

I ran back to the phone. "I can go. I'll be ready at eight thirty."

By eight fifteen on Saturday morning I was dressed with my bathing suit under my clothes, had a towel looped over my shoulders, and was sitting on my front doorstep waiting for Christina and her father to arrive. It was already getting warm, and it felt like a perfect beach day.

When their car pulled up, I trotted out, let myself into the backseat, and sat there grinning. Christina and her father stared at me like I'd turned purple.

"Sarah, where's your suitcase?" Christina blurted out.

41

Suitcase? It turned out the beach wasn't fifteen minutes from our neighborhood, or even thirty minutes or an hour. It was three and a half hours, its name was Ocean City because it was full of tall hotels, and we'd be staying overnight in one of the tall hotels because Mr. Perez knew the manager and had gotten two rooms for free. I said they'd better come inside so I could ask my parents all over again, since when I'd said "swimming," they probably thought we were going to a pool.

While Mr. Perez and Christina talked to my mom and dad, I ran upstairs. I dumped my schoolbooks out of my backpack and threw some clothes, another bathing suit, and my toothbrush into it. I was hoping they'd still say yes, since Mr. Perez had already driven over to pick me up.

I listened at the top of the steps.

"It will be nice for Christina to have a friend with her," Mr. Perez was saying.

Yes! I ran down the steps and nearly tripped over Christina, who was on her way up.

During the drive we played a game with the license plates on the cars we passed, where we had to figure out what the letters on the plate stood for. Like PSC was "Pretty Stinky Cat" and YQB was "You Quit Burping." We laughed the whole way to the beach.

I could see why they call it Ocean City. It was the most crowded beach I've ever seen, with cars stuck in jams along the roads, and high-rise hotels over our heads. On the sand it was crowded, too, but we managed to find a place to lay our towels near the beach volleyball net, in between a group of high school girls drinking sodas and a family with three little sand-covered kids.

By then it was really hot, and Christina and I ran right down to the water. But before we even touched it with our toes, I heard Mr. Perez calling us.

"Oh, right," said Christina. "You haven't heard the riptide story yet."

"The what?"

"Come on." She led me back toward our towels. "Just listen to the story and let him know you understand. Then we can go swimming."

"Miss Sarah," said Mr. Perez. "Do you know what it is, a riptide?"

The way he rolled his *r* it sounded like it was an exotic summer drink with maybe ginger ale and guava juice, but I didn't want to guess wrong, so I just shook my head.

"It is very dangerous," he said. He pointed to the ocean, which, I must admit, had bigger waves than the beach we used to go to in Portland. He explained how a riptide is a really strong current that can grab you and whisk you out into the ocean so fast you don't even have time to yell "Help!" He said he got caught in one once when he was a young boy. "There is only one way to survive a riptide," he said. He raised his eyebrows at me, and his dark eyes sparkled just like Christina's do.

I realized he was waiting for me to ask him what that one way is, so I said, "What's that?"

"You have to let it take you all the way out to its end. Then you can swim around it and come back in. If you fight against it and try to swim straight to shore, you will drown."

I laughed. "You're kidding, right? Boy, if I had a current trying to take me out to sea, I'd just swim like crazy to get back in."

Mr. Perez got a worried look on his face. "That's exactly how people die in riptides," he said. "They fight and swim as hard as they can until they have no strength left. You cannot outswim a riptide."

I looked from him to Christina. "Do they have riptides here, or is this just an El Salvador thing?"

Mr. Perez shook his head. "This is why I am telling you! They could have one right here." He pointed to the ocean, which was looking rougher by the minute.

"But Papa," said Christina calmly, "last year the lifeguard told me they almost never have them at this beach, and that if they see one they'll warn all the swimmers."

Mr. Perez nodded. "I just want you to be careful," he said.

We walked back to the water. "Don't worry," said Christina. "I've heard the riptide story about a hundred times, so I'll tell you what to do if we get caught in one."

At that point I was thinking maybe we should just swim in the pool at our hotel, but Christina added, "You know the best way to stay out of a riptide?"

I said no, but I certainly would like to know.

"Stay in the shallow water," she said.

That sounded like a great idea to me, especially since the waves close to shore were lots of fun to jump over and dive into and flop onto and splash at each other.

Instead of going to a restaurant for dinner we went to the boardwalk, and Mr. Perez bought us pizza from one shop, ice cream from another, and saltwater taffy from the last shop we walked past, yawning, on our way to our hotel.

Christina and I jumped on our bed for a while before we settled down to go to sleep.

"Do you think you could really do the right thing in a riptide—not fight it, I mean?" I asked her in the dark.

It was quiet while she was thinking. "My father says it's really hard not to just panic and swim for shore," she said. "You have to be very brave to let it take you out into the ocean."

I sighed. "Let's stay in the shallow water again tomorrow, okay?"

"Sure," she said.

The beach looked normal, except for the fact that everyone was wearing their winter boots, which should have tipped me off right there. Anyway, I didn't know where Christina was, but like an idiot I marched right down to the water and dived in. Right away I was in over my head, and all of a sudden, *whoosh!* This thing like a water-powered superhighway zipped me out so far that the people on shore looked like ants wearing winter boots. So what did I do? Did I relax and float and let it take me out to sea so I could swim around it? No! I kicked and paddled and struggled like a maniac. I couldn't get any closer to shore, and I was getting more and more tired until I just didn't have any strength left. Finally I gave up and sank down under the water. Everything was this eerie bluish-green, and I knew I was about to drown, so I woke up.

I was so scared I was sweating all over. Christina

was sound asleep, and it was still dark out. I went to the bathroom to splash cold water on my face. It was simple, I told myself. I had disobeyed one of the basic rules of dreaming: Don't go near the dangerous stuff, or the dream will turn into a nightmare. I promised myself I'd be much more careful for the rest of the night and went back to bed.

We had a great time again at the ocean the next day. We collected shells and built a castle, and when we went into the water I made sure my toes were touching sand every second!

SIX

I put some of the shells we collected on top of my dresser for decoration, and some of them I left in my backpack so I could carry them around as a souvenir of the trip.

At school on Monday, Mr. Harrison was nice to me. I was glad to find out he didn't hold a grudge.

We started our science project about insects and their life cycles. Christina, Jamal, Kelly, and I got to go to the woods next to the school and gather leaves, rotting wood, dirt, and pine cones for our insect house. Then we took these white wormy things out of a box marked LARVAE and put them in with the dirt and other stuff. They were going to become some kind of bug, but that part would be a surprise. We were supposed to watch and see where they liked living best—in the leaves, dirt, rotten wood, or pine cones.

Mr. Harrison told us lots of things about larvae, like how they sit around eating and growing all day and shed their skins when they get too big for them. Then he told us the weirdest thing. He said that some people who live in the South American rain-forest actually eat insect larvae. Everyone in the class groaned and almost threw up when we heard that. He said they taste like soft cheese. We all groaned again, and Kelly asked him how he knew. Mr. Harrison said he learned it on the Discovery Channel. Kelly poked me and whispered, "Do you think he tasted one of our larvae?" I punched her in the arm and told her to shush because I know Mr. Harrison wouldn't do anything like that.

I did a great job of ignoring Eric whenever he was around. It was starting to look like he would forget all about me and pick on somebody else. "He's not worth getting mad at," Christina said. "He's not your friend and he's not in your family." I decided as long as he stayed out of my face, I'd stay out of his.

On Thursday, I went to Christina's after school and met her older brother, Antonio. He was eating a sandwich and watching television in the den. Christina introduced us, and he actually stood up politely until we left the room.

Antonio works at the hospital, sometimes the day shift and sometimes the night shift. He didn't come to the United States until he was twelve, so he has a Spanish accent all the time. Christina lost hers, just like she said she would, and she sounds like the other kids in class. The funny thing is, they all think *I* have an accent! I think it's weird that they can't even hear their own accents.

Christina dropped her backpack on the kitchen table and rolled up her sleeves. "Want to help me with the dishes?" she asked. "My mom lets me leave them in the morning so I won't be late for school, as long as I have them done before she and my dad get home from work."

We scraped off plates with half-eaten tortillas and bits of scrambled egg on them, wiped grease out of the big iron skillet, and stuck everything in the sink to soak. Antonio came in with his dishes. "Here you go. Just in case you didn't have enough work to do." He handed them to Christina and went back to the den.

"I wish I had a sister," said Christina. "Then I'd have some help with my chores."

"Jerod does the pots and pans and I load the dishwasher," I said. "What does Antonio do?"

"He eats and makes a big fat mess, that's what my brother does," she said real loud so Antonio could hear. Then more quietly she said, "My mother is an old-fashioned Salvadoran. She thinks girls clean up and boys don't."

"You mean he doesn't have to help?" I could hardly believe it. I'd throw a fit if I had to do one bit more work than Jerod does around our house.

"He doesn't lift a finger," Christina said loudly again. "And he'll go into shock when he marries an American and he has to learn to scrub the floors and change diapers!" She was giggling as Antonio appeared around the corner.

"I will not go into shock. I'll just tell her I'm the boss and she has to clean the house to make me happy."

Christina loaded up a sponge with soapy water and splashed it onto Antonio's arm. "And she'll throw you out on the street!" she cried.

Antonio laughed and grabbed Christina's wrists.

Christina squealed. "Quick, Sarah, get the sprayer!"

But Antonio got it first and sprayed Christina right in the face. She was laughing so hard I thought she would choke on the water. She got hold of a Brillo pad and stuffed it down the back of Antonio's shirt. Antonio wriggled and tugged at his shirt until the Brillo pad fell out.

I decided to join in the fun, so I picked up a ladle full of soapy water and tossed it toward Antonio, but I missed and it sloshed onto the floor. He grabbed each of us by one arm so we couldn't move.

"Two against one and you still lose. You see? Men are superior!"

Christina chanted in a singsong voice, "Antonio is going to change the diapers if he doesn't want to have a divorce."

He let go of us and started to unbutton his shirt. "I've got to go to work. Christina, you wash and iron my shirt and clean up this mess before Mama gets home."

"Antonio's going to change the diapers," Christina chanted again.

He tickled her armpit and she jumped away. "If I didn't have to go to work . . ." he chided, wagging one finger at us. He tossed his shirt at Christina. She caught it and plopped it in a heap on a chair.

"If you didn't have to go to work, we'd teach you how to clean up the kitchen," she said.

He rolled his eyes at her, then leaned over and kissed her on the cheek. "Tell Mama I'll be home by midnight, okay?"

"I will," she said.

After he left, we mopped the floor, washed the dishes, and wiped the counters. Then Christina picked up Antonio's shirt. "If I have to wash this one, I might as well do a whole load."

My eyes got wide. "You're not really going to wash and iron it for him, are you?"

She looked at the label. "No," she said. "It's permanent press."

I went downstairs with her while she put in a load of laundry. She explained to me how her mother believed she was preparing Christina for marriage by teaching her to do all the housework.

"Doesn't it make you mad?" I asked.

Christina shrugged. "Sometimes. But it's the way she was brought up. It's part of her. Being mad at her about it would be like getting mad at someone because you don't like their nose."

That made sense to me. But I'm just glad my mom thinks Jerod should wash the pots and pans every night and scour the bathroom sinks every other week.

SEVEN

Christina taught me soccer moves every chance we got, after school and on the weekend, so by the time my recess detention was over with I was getting to be a pretty good player. That next Monday, I finally got to play soccer, and I scored a goal in my first game.

On Tuesday when my mom got home from work, she and I walked over to Christina's so our moms could meet. They drank coffee together and talked while Christina and I took Tito for a walk in the backyard. He didn't really walk, though—he kind of ran in circles, and we ran after him so he wouldn't get lost.

Christina was allowed to come to my house after that, so we made plans for Saturday. She would come over and my mom would drive us to Wheaton Plaza. We decided that one of our stops at the mall would be the photo booth to get pictures of the two of us together. I picked out a place on my wall especially for pictures of me and my new best friend, Christina.

On Wednesday morning Jamal, Kelly, Christina, and I examined our insect larvae. They were still squirmy and pale—no signs of turning into another kind of bug yet. Jamal picked one up with a stick and held it in my face. "Sarah, you like cheese, don't you? Have a taste." But when I opened my mouth and pretended I was going to eat it, Jamal got scared and put it back in its house real quick. Sometimes boys are so squeamish.

We did find out that our larvae like to live in rotting wood. The four of us wrote up our science observation paper, and Mr. Harrison thought we did such a great job that he put our names up on the Super Achievers board.

By Thursday, I was having a terrific week. That was before Eric stopped ignoring me.

There was a thunderstorm during lunch. After it had passed, the teachers decided that even though everything was wet we could still go outside for recess. They told us to keep our feet dry, but I don't know how they expected us to do that with puddles in the blacktop potholes.

I didn't mind getting my feet wet. What I minded was what Eric did.

While I was bent over tying my sneaker, I felt a

shove. I fell over and landed right on my rump in a puddle. I looked up into Eric's grinning face.

When I stood up, I had a big dirty wet spot on the seat of my jeans. Eric started laughing like it was the funniest thing he'd ever seen. "Sarah wet her pants!"

A couple of fourth graders cracked up. I scowled at them and they ran away.

But Eric wouldn't stop. "Look, everybody, Sarah wet her pants!" He shouted it like he was Paul Revere or something.

I could feel my face flush hot pink. "Shut up, you creep!" I was so mad I wanted to shove his head into a pothole.

"Poor Sarah, she's so embarrassed that she wet her pants," he bellowed.

By now half the kids on the playground had heard him, and most of them were laughing. I started toward Eric with one fist ready for his face.

"Uh-oh. Sarah's going to have detention all year for fighting," he mocked me.

At that moment Christina grabbed my arm and yanked me away from him. "Don't let him make you mad," she said in my ear. She tied her jacket around my waist.

The playground aide finally figured out there was a fight going on and told us to spread out or she was going to send us all inside. Christina led me to the jungle gym.

"He is such a jerk!" she said.

"I'm going to kill him," I said. I think there was smoke coming out of my ears.

"You've let him make you mad," she said.

"Wouldn't this make *you* mad?" I screeched.

Christina sat down on one of the low bars. "Well, yeah . . . but that's what he wanted you to do. By getting mad you're letting him win."

I narrowed my eyes. "I am *not* going to let him win," I said slowly.

"Good. So you're going to ignore him and you won't get in trouble again and we can keep playing soccer during recess, right?" She looked at me hopefully.

"Nope," I said. "I'm going to get him back—but *good*."

Christina groaned.

"I won't get caught—I promise," I assured her.

She gave me a doubtful look. "I think you're wasting your time on a stupid boy who just likes to make you mad. He's not worth it."

"I'm not going to let him get away with this," I said simply.

I untied her jacket from around my waist and offered it back to her.

"That's okay," she said. "It'll hide the spot until you get home." She looked toward the field. "Let's go get in on the soccer game—it might be your last chance, you know," she said with her eyes wide so I'd get the message.

I did get the message, and it made me more determined than ever to both get Eric good and not get caught.

EIGHT

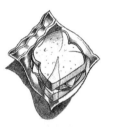

The nice thing about having a dad who's a carpenter is that he builds great stuff for you. When I was little, he built me a playhouse with two windows, a play sink, and a door that opened and shut on hinges. Here in Maryland he'd already made some awesome bookshelves for my room. The only *problem* with having a dad who is a carpenter is that when there aren't enough people calling him to work on their houses, he will probably start to tear up your house.

When I got home from school on Thursday, our kitchen looked like a bulldozer had run through it. My dad's legs and belly stuck out from under one of the ripped-up cabinets.

"You didn't like the old ones?" I asked, eyeing the damage.

"Figured oak would be better than pine," came the voice from the cabinet. Then I heard the loud *rrriiippp* of another nail being wrenched out. "How was school?"

"Okay." I'm not very good at hiding my feelings, so as soon as I said "Okay," the rest of my dad appeared from under the cabinet.

"What's wrong? What happened?" he asked. "Whose jacket is that?"

"Christina's." I decided to answer the easiest question first.

"And . . . ?" My dad looked at me expectantly and brushed sawdust off his face.

I plopped onto the floor next to him. "*And* I have to wash it for her because it's messed up with dirt from my pants, which got that way because there's a kid at my school who hates me."

"He hates you, so he put dirt on your pants?"

"He pushed me into dirty water." I clarified the situation for him.

My dad tapped his hammer on his thigh. "And you probably want my advice on what you should do about this kid who hates you, right?"

I shook my head. "Nope. I already decided what to do. I'm going to get revenge."

"Sarah, that's a lousy idea!" He went on and gave me two lectures, one on "Walking Away from Conflict" and the other on "Staying Out of Trouble at School." I played with a little pile of sawdust and listened. I mostly agreed with what he said. It's just that I did plan on staying out of trouble at school, because I didn't plan to get caught.

When he was done, I said, "Thanks, Dad," and went downstairs to put Christina's jacket in the wash.

The next morning when I woke up I was hardly even angry at Eric anymore. I'm that way with anger sometimes. I can go to bed furious and wake up the next day ready to forget all about it. It's like sleeping is a "time out" and I calm down. I decided to skip the whole revenge thing and "Walk Away from Conflict," just like my dad told me to do.

Mr. Harrison took us to the media center and we each got to pick out two books for Drop Everything and Read time. While the class was still milling around choosing books, Mr. Harrison tapped me on the shoulder. "Sarah, Ms. Ortiz has a book I meant to pick up from her—poems and pictures her class put together. Would you please go get it for me?"

I was glad Mr. Harrison gave me an errand to do for him. I think he was trying to show me that we were getting along again and that he knew he could trust me. The only problem was, Ms. Ortiz was a sixth-grade teacher. Eric's sixth-grade teacher. And I was determined to steer clear of Eric for the rest of my life.

I didn't get far before I met Ms. Ortiz and her whole lined-up class coming down the hall in the other direction. I told her what Mr. Harrison needed, and she said, "It's sitting right on my desk waiting for him. You know where my classroom is, right?" I nodded. "Go ahead and pick it up, then, sweetie." She waved her class along.

I looked at the floor and hurried, but Eric had already seen me.

"Hey, Sarah, did you wet your pants again today? Nah. I think she pooped in them this time—pee-yew!" He held his nose and the rest of the sixth graders cracked up.

Ms. Ortiz yelled at Eric, "No talking in line, Mr. Bardo!" But she didn't say, "No humiliating the fifth graders" or "No being horribly obnoxious to the new girl" or "No embarrassing Sarah in front of everyone."

I felt my face turn red and hot. I was furious all over again—even more furious than I'd been on the playground. Getting laughed at by all those kids was worse than having to take off my clothes in the doctor's office. And half of them probably thought I really had messed my pants.

I marched to Ms. Ortiz's room. I stood there staring at the book of poems on her desk. The cover said *We Are Poets, Too* and had a computer picture of a blue and pink butterfly on a yellow daisy. The room was quiet. The one fluorescent light they'd left on buzzed like a mosquito. I could put dirt in Eric's desk. I could mash the banana from my lunch and smear it on the seat of his chair. I could fill his cubby with wet paper towels. I could . . . My imagination was working overtime, but everything I thought of doing would have gotten me in big trouble because it would have been obvious who had been in the room alone while the class was gone. Then I had a brilliant idea.

I left the poetry book on Ms. Ortiz's desk and tip-toed three doors down to my own classroom. I opened the box we kept our science experiment in. "Sorry, little guys," I whispered to the four squirmy larvae I pulled out. I closed them in my hand and sneaked back to Ms. Ortiz's room.

Eric's cubby was easy to find. So was his lunch. I opened his lunchbox and unzipped the zip-lock bag that held his sandwich.

Just then I heard footsteps in the hallway. I froze. I didn't even breathe. The sound got closer. I ducked behind some jackets hanging on hooks. The foot-steps came right up to the classroom, then kept going down the hall. *Whew!* Quickly I opened the sandwich—bologna and cheese—and arranged the pale larvae on it like an extra garnish. They wiggled like lively fat noodles. I closed everything back up, grabbed the poetry book, and rushed back to the media center.

Mr. Harrison had us sit at the library tables while he showed us Ms. Ortiz's book. Each kid in her class had written a poem on the computer and made a colored computer picture to go along with the poem. Eric's was about frogs with a green frog on a yellow lily pad. Mr. Harrison said we were going to do a book just like it, so we should start thinking about our poems. All I could think about was how frogs eat insects—just like Eric was about to.

As we got closer to lunchtime, I got more and more excited. I was bursting to tell Christina what a great trick I'd played. But I knew the only way this would be the perfect crime was if I kept my mouth shut.

Since fifth and sixth graders eat at opposite ends of the lunchroom, with fourth graders in between, I decided to throw some trash away right after lunch started and walk all the way down to the other end of the room to do it. I wanted to see what Eric was eating.

I walked close to Eric's table. He'd already opened his lunchbox and was eating his cookies first. The zip-lock bag holding his sandwich was lying on the table. I took about one step every ten seconds, staring, waiting, watching Eric talk with his mouth full. Then he did it. He opened the bag and pulled out his sandwich. But he didn't take a bite. Instead he grabbed a potato chip from another kid's lunch and threw it in the kid's face.

I must have looked like a zombie staring like that with my mouth open, waiting for Eric to start on his sandwich. "Come on, do it," I said under my breath. He lifted up the sandwich and took a huge bite.

"Oh, gross!" I said out loud.

The sixth-grade girls at the table next to me looked up. A girl with about thirty ebony braids and a red bead at the end of each one said, "What's *your* problem?"

I was afraid they would think I was the weirdo again, so I explained. "Eric Bardo is eating bugs."

Eric had just swallowed his first mouthful and was sinking his teeth into the sandwich again.

The girl with the braids called out, "Hey, Eric, she says you're eating bugs." A couple of the girls got up to get a good look at Eric's food.

"Who says that?" Eric looked around and caught sight of me. "Oh, her. That's because she poops in her pants!" He chugged some milk and then laughed until milk came out of his nose.

I walked right up to him. "You *are* eating bugs, you creep."

By now the whole table of sixth-grade girls was on their feet, gathered around Eric's table. I knew it was only seconds before a teacher would yell at us to get back to our seats, and I wanted everyone to know I was right and Eric was wrong. "Look in your sandwich if you don't believe me," I said.

Eric scoffed and opened his sandwich. Two wriggly larvae fell onto the lunch table.

Eric screamed and jumped up. The sixth-grade girls screamed. The guys at Eric's table hooted and gagged. A tall, angry teacher grabbed me by the collar. I guess she figured if I was the only one not gagging or screaming, I must be part of the problem. But when she saw Eric's open sandwich with a plump larva still wriggling on it, she let go of my collar, covered her mouth with her hand, and ran out of the cafeteria.

So much for the perfect crime. I was led away to the principal's office by a teacher with a strong stomach. I'm surprised they didn't handcuff me.

Our principal, Dr. Enomoto, hardly knew what to say. I don't think "Larvae Smuggling" is in her rule book.

"Our teacher said they taste good—like soft cheese," I said. I hoped that maybe she'd believe I was doing something nice for Eric instead of something awful. "Eric already had cheese on his bologna. I just added a little more."

66

I don't think Dr. Enomoto liked my excuse, because she looked very grouchy when she called Mr. Harrison on the intercom to come and get me. Mr. Harrison was really mad because I had betrayed his trust and done such a terrible thing (and, I think, because he had to give up the rest of his lunch period to yell at me). Jamal and Kelly were really mad because I'd wasted most of our science project. Christina didn't even speak to me because of most of the reasons I already mentioned, plus the fact that I got recess detention for the whole next week.

The afternoon was pretty weird. Jamal, Kelly, and Christina were stonefaced and quiet, so during math when we were in our seats facing one another, I felt all squirmy like I didn't want to be there. I decided to see if I could get Christina's attention if I tried hard enough.

"Christina, would you walk home with me so I can talk to you?" I whispered.

She stared harder at her math problems.

I tapped her on the arm, but she pulled it away like I'd hurt her.

"Christina, I need to tell you what *he* did!" I pleaded.

She yanked her math book and notepad onto her lap and turned her seat so her back was to me.

I sighed and glanced at Kelly and Jamal. They

were glaring at me. I bent my head over my work and tried to concentrate.

But when we left the classroom to go to gym, a bunch of guys from the other fifth grade spotted me in the hallway and called out, "Way to go, Sarah!" and high-fived me. They laughed and called me the Larvae Meister and the Lunch Bug Queen like I was some kind of hero to have stood up to Eric Bardo. It was kind of fun, but it wasn't worth having lost my best friend.

That evening Mr. Harrison called my parents. They yelled at me for a while and then grounded me for the whole weekend. That meant I couldn't go to the mall with Christina to get our pictures taken in the photo booth, which didn't really matter because she wasn't speaking to me anyway.

Jerod was the only person who wasn't mad at me. Just before bedtime I knocked on his bedroom door. I needed to talk to someone who wouldn't glare at me.

"Wassup?"

"Can I come in?" I asked.

"Eup."

I sat in his office chair. He was in bed reading a biology book. Jerod has this great desk with bookshelves and a study lamp and a swivel chair with wheels—and he does his homework in bed.

He looked at me over his book. "You're not staying out of trouble too well, huh?"

That was the understatement of the year. With all the hollering and lecturing going on around our house, Jerod knew the whole story.

"Yeah. Mom and Dad are pretty upset."

"I didn't mean in trouble with them."

"Well, yeah, my teacher is pretty mad, too."

Jerod shook his head. "I'm not talking about trouble with him, either."

I gave Jerod a quizzical look. "You mean with Christina and my work group?"

"Nope. Those folks are no trouble at all." He flipped through his biology book, waiting for me to beg him to tell me what in the world he was talking about.

I couldn't stand it. "Jerod, everyone is being mean to me and now you are too!" I was ready to cry.

"I am not. I'm just warning you that you're in trouble, that's all."

"With *who?*" My voice cracked.

"Eric."

In all the commotion and yelling and punishing, I'd overlooked something very basic. I felt the blood drain from my face. My hands got clammy.

"Eup," said Jerod. "Now he's going to get you back."

NINE

On Saturday morning I called Christina's house to let her know we wouldn't be going to the mall. I was hoping maybe she had cooled off overnight and would be willing to talk to me. But Antonio answered the phone and said she'd gone to the mall with a friend.

"That's *me* she was supposed to go with, and I'm calling to say I can't go," I said.

"She's already gone," he said.

"How can she go to the mall with me if I can't go?" I asked.

"I don't know," said Antonio.

I could tell I wasn't going to get any further with him, so I just said to tell her I'd called, then hung up.

I think Jerod ended up being sorry he'd warned me about Eric. I bugged him all weekend long: "Jerod, how bad does a broken nose hurt?" "Jerod, do you think Mom and Dad will let me transfer to a private school?" "Jerod, would you be my body-guard? All you have to do is come back to elementary school." "Jerod, how can I get the flu real bad by Monday morning?" And finally, "Jerod, would you teach me karate?"

He actually agreed to that last request. Maybe it was only to shut me up, but on Sunday afternoon I got karate lessons.

He taught me how to concentrate and put all my strength into my hand or foot—whatever I'd be using to hit my opponent. And he showed me how to do a jab and a knife hand and jump into the air to do a side kick just like Bruce Lee. Then to see how well I'd learned everything, he said we could do a pretend fight.

But when I jumped into the air to get him with a side kick, he grabbed my foot. I landed on my back with a crash, got the wind knocked out of me, hit my head on the floor, and slammed my elbow so hard I thought I'd broken my arm.

Jerod stood over me looking worried. "You were supposed to watch out for my defense move," he said. He doesn't really enjoy hurting me the way he used to when we were younger.

"Right," I said, holding my elbow and wincing. "Can you go get Dad? I need to go to the emergency room."

My dad rubbed my elbow, which made it hurt more, but he showed me how I could move my arm. He said I wouldn't be able to do that if it were broken.

After a few minutes everything hurt a little less and I felt like maybe I'd be normal again without going to the hospital. Fortunately Dad didn't ask why Jerod was teaching me karate. He just waited until I felt better and then went back to tearing up the kitchen.

I tried calling Christina again, but her mother said she was doing her homework and couldn't come to the phone. I left another message that I'd called, but I was starting to get the picture that she wasn't going to call me back.

After dinner I got out the thermometer and took my temperature. I thought maybe—just maybe—I felt the flu coming on. Ninety-eight point six. It crossed my mind to hold the thermometer up to my lamp to make the mercury go higher. I did that once when I was about seven and my mom almost had a heart attack when she read one hundred six point four. She was ready to pack me in ice and call an ambulance, but my dad took my temperature again without leaving the room. It was only ninety-nine. I decided not to try that trick again.

I got myself to bed on time. (I'd been doing pretty

much everything like a perfect child all weekend.) But then I couldn't sleep. In the dark quiet of my bedroom the stuff I'd been scared about all day—going to school the next morning—felt a lot more scary.

When I got up for my eighth drink of water and to pee for the third time, I noticed all the lights were off. Dad and Mom were already snoring. I'm not used to being the only one up, so it was a strange feeling, but it meant that I could do whatever I wanted. I went downstairs and watched an old movie about a blob from outer space—which was much less terrifying than Eric Bardo—until I couldn't keep my eyes open anymore.

My mom had to shake me awake the next morning. When I finally realized where I was and what day it was, it felt like I was waking up into a nightmare instead of out of one.

I took my temperature again. This time it was below normal. I felt my arm again, hoping maybe it was broken after all. It was sore, but I could still move it. I checked my skin for chickenpox, looked out the window to see if there had been a very early snowstorm, and finally gave up and got dressed.

As I walked to school, I kept glancing behind me just to make sure Eric wasn't there, ready to attack.

When I walked into our classroom, Christina took one look at me and turned away. Mr. Harrison gave us a language arts assignment to find dictionary definitions for a list of spelling words. It's pretty hard to ignore someone when you have to work with them in a cooperative learning group, but that's basically what Christina, Kelly, and Jamal did. We took turns with the writing and the dictionary, but they hardly talked to me. It was like the three of them were a team and I was a shadow.

I was already feeling very lousy when we got to the word *gymnast.*

"Hey, Christina," said Kelly, "that's just like the gymnasts we saw performing at the mall."

"Yeah," said Christina.

I felt like a balloon that just had all its air leak out.

Jamal shoved the dictionary in front of me.

"The word is *foreign,*" he said.

I looked down at the open dictionary. My eyes were full of tears and one big one plopped onto the page. I wiped it off real quick. I wanted to ask Christina if they'd gotten their pictures taken at the photo booth and if she had photos of her and Kelly on her wall now, but I couldn't stand to know.

"Come on, Sarah. The other groups are ahead of us," Jamal whined at me.

"Oh, I'll do it." Kelly pulled the dictionary away and looked up *foreign.*

I wasn't any help to my group after that.

I had detention for lunch and recess both. I guess they decided I was a danger to anyone in the cafeteria who didn't want extra garnishes on their food. I was actually glad to be in detention because it meant I didn't have to sit by myself at lunch and also that Eric couldn't get to me.

The afternoon wasn't any better than the morning because my work group was still treating me like a criminal, and on my way to gym those fifth-grade boys had forgotten all about me being a hero.

I decided I'd corner Christina on her way home and *make* her talk to me. When we lined up to go home, she was way ahead of me. And when we piled into the hall, I tried to catch up with her, but she hurried away. Outside I searched for her in the crowd of kids pouring out the front doors. There she was, climbing onto Kelly's bus with her.

Right when I felt like things couldn't get any worse, Eric appeared. He marched right up to me. He crumpled most of the front of my shirt into his fist and sneered in my face. "You're dead meat," he growled.

I ran all the way home. Jerod was in the driveway shooting hoops by himself.

"Wassup, Sarah?"

I threw my backpack onto the lawn. "How much cash do you have?" I shouted. I was panting and half-crying. "I'll pay you back, I promise." I wiped sweat off my face with my sleeve. "I'm going back to Portland *right now!*" That's when I really started bawling—as soon as I said Portland—because it felt like home, and this new place felt scary and lonely.

Jerod was eyeing me like I'd gone off the deep end. "Geez, Sarah. Where are you going to live in Portland?"

"With Andrea," I sobbed. At that point I figured I really should have written to her, but it was a little late.

"How are you going to get to the airport?" Jerod wanted to know.

"I don't know!" I screeched. I didn't want to figure out all the little details. I just wanted to leave Maryland immediately.

I must have had snot running out of my nose, I was crying so hard, because Jerod went inside to get a roll of toilet paper and then handed it to me. I blew my nose.

"Why do you want to leave?" he asked.

I told him the whole story of my work group being mean to me because I'd fed our science project to Eric, Christina being best friends with Kelly now because I was always in detention or grounded, and Eric being madder than ever and probably planning to beat me to a pulp.

Jerod sat on the grass and listened. "I've got an idea," he said when I was done. He disappeared into the house.

I figured he realized the danger I was in, knew where Mom's credit cards were, and was going to buy me a plane ticket and a taxi ride to the airport. Instead he came out with a bed pillow.

"I think they've already got extra pillows at Andrea's house," I said.

He shook his head. "They taught us this in school." He handed me the basketball. "Dribble it on the driveway."

I pouted. I wasn't exactly in the mood to play basketball. But Jerod had been awfully nice to listen to me blubber for so long, so I dribbled the ball a minute.

"See, the ball is bouncing back because the driveway is a hard surface. And you can keep bouncing it because it comes back to your hands," Jerod said as if I needed an explanation.

I caught the ball and held it. "How is this supposed to help me get to Portland?"

"Hang on." He dropped the pillow onto the driveway. "Now dribble the ball on the pillow."

I rolled my eyes, but I did what he said. At least I tried to do it. I tossed the ball onto the pillow, but instead of bouncing back to my hands, it just landed with a soft plop and rolled onto the driveway.

"Try again," he said.

I threw the ball harder, but it wouldn't bounce.

"Again," Jerod urged me.

I heaved the ball at the pillow. It bounced about two inches and rolled away.

"Do it again," Jerod ordered.

"No!" I yelled. "It doesn't work and it's boring!"

"Exactly!" Jerod was so excited I thought he was about to hug me. "It doesn't work and it's boring. That's why you don't want to do it anymore."

I stared at him. "They teach you really dumb stuff at your school, Jerod."

"They're teaching us how to stay out of fights. If you fight back, you're like the hard driveway." He dribbled the ball to show me. "You keep bouncing the ball up into the other guy's hands, so he'll keep bouncing— or fighting—with you. The best way to get someone to stop fighting with you is to act like a pillow."

I raised one eyebrow. "Act like a pillow?"

"Yeah." He tossed the ball at the pillow. It thudded and sat there. "It's no fun if the ball doesn't bounce. The person you were fighting with will get bored and walk away."

I sniffled. "And how am I supposed to act like a pillow, exactly?"

"You don't fight back. You don't do anything— like the pillow, see?"

We both looked at the pillow. It was lying on the driveway doing nothing.

"Eric will get bored and leave you alone," said Jerod.

"You're sure about this?"

Jerod nodded. "It was a guest speaker who told us."

I sat down hard on the grass. "Eric is *really* mad. He's not going to leave me alone."

"Not yet," said Jerod. "He has to try the first bounce."

My stomach lurched. It sounded like something from a science fiction movie. "The first bounce?" I asked in a small voice.

"Yeah. He'll do something really awful to you. After that is when you act like a pillow."

I felt very queasy. "Couldn't we just pool our money and buy me a ticket to Portland?" I begged.

He didn't have a chance to answer because Mom pulled her car into the driveway with the backseat full of grocery bags. Jerod's job is to carry the bags in and my job is to help Mom put the food away, so we both had to get busy.

"You might want to take your pillow back inside," said Jerod as he hoisted two bags into his arms.

"*My* pillow?" My eyes bugged out. I lifted it off

the driveway and held it away from me. It was a mess with dirt and tar.

"Sarah, what on earth did you do to your pillow?" Mom snatched it away. "You take care of the groceries. I'll have to get stain remover on this right away." She shook her head and looked at me crossly.

It seemed like no matter how hard I tried, every time I turned around I was in trouble again.

TEN

Jerod's basketball lesson didn't make me any less afraid of what Eric was going to do to me next. But I did stop planning what I would do to him after that. Pillows don't make plans for revenge.

Waiting for him to try the first bounce was really getting to me. I felt like walking up to him and saying, "Would you please break my nose so I can ignore you and we can stop this feud once and for all?" I didn't, though.

Mr. Harrison bought more larvae for our group, so Jamal and Kelly started being nicer to me. But Christina was still giving me the silent treatment, which was driving me crazy. Finally I told her so.

"I'm not talking to you because I'm angry with you," she said, and turned her head away.

"You're angry at me for fighting with Eric, right?"

I watched the back of her head nod.

"Well, I'm not going to fight him anymore," I

said. I started to tell her about Jerod's advice, but Mr. Harrison came by and asked how our math problems were going.

"Fine," we answered in unison.

When he went off to talk to another group, Christina hissed at me in a whisper, "You care more about Eric than you do about me!"

My mouth dropped wide open at that one. Then my whole face screwed up into one big question mark. "What?!" I forgot to whisper.

"You spend all your time on him—fighting with him, planning revenge on him, being punished for doing bad things to him—you have no time left to do anything with me. You can't eat lunch with me, you can't play soccer with me during recess, you can't do stuff with me on the weekends—*nothing!*"

I stared down at the numbers on my paper. All this time I'd thought I was the one being left out, but Christina felt left out, too. It made me more determined than ever to get out of the feud with Eric.

"I'm *really* not going to fight with him anymore," I said. I tried to make it sound very convincing.

Christina gave me a sad look. "I don't believe you," she said.

Mr. Harrison came by again, and that was the end of our conversation. I realized the only way to convince Christina I wasn't fighting with Eric anymore would be to prove it to her. And to do that, all I could do was wait.

As it turned out, I didn't have to wait very long.

I stayed after school to check out a couple of books from the media center. With no one to hang out with and no homework left after recess detention, I'd been doing a lot of reading. After I got the books, I walked across the playground toward home, past the after-school day-care kids who were playing with some lady's golden retriever. As I crossed the street and started down the sidewalk, I heard an eerie singsong voice call my name. I looked around.

"Oh, Sa-rah," came the voice again.

This time I recognized it. Eric was trying to sound like the Ghost of Christmas Past.

"Oh, Saaa-raaah," came another voice from a different direction. That was one thing I hadn't counted on—getting beat up by a whole gang of boys. I froze.

They stepped out: Roger from behind a clump of bushes in his front yard, Eric from Roger's porch, and Lawrence from behind the house next to Roger's. All three of them were holding guns.

I felt the blood drain from my cheeks. I was too terrified to move or even scream. I definitely hadn't counted on Eric *killing* me.

"Ha-ha. She thinks they're real guns!" Eric definitely got a kick out of the panicked expression on my face.

I started to breathe again. They came closer and surrounded me. They got close enough so I could see the yellow scum on Roger's teeth and the Kool-Aid stains on the front of Lawrence's huge lime green sweatshirt.

"They're water guns," Eric said, and the three of them cracked up.

I was actually disappointed. "Give me a break, Eric. Do you think I'll freak if I get a little wet?"

The three of them were grinning strangely. All three guns were pointed at me.

"It's not water," said Eric slowly.

My stomach tightened slightly as my brain shuffled through the possibilities of what else it could be. Vinegar? Better keep my eyes closed. Soap? Ditto. Something smelly, like rotten tomato juice? . . . Suddenly I saw the disgusting smiles on their faces and realized what it must be—what it *had* to be.

I screamed and ran.

Eric shouted "Fire!"

I felt the spray on my back and legs. It hit my head and soaked into my hair. It smelled like wet diapers. I screamed all the way to my house.

In my room I yanked my clothes off and stuffed

them into a plastic bag. Then I ran to the shower and washed my hair three times. Once I was dressed in clean clothes, I filled the bathtub with water and dumped my wet clothes in to soak, along with my sneakers.

While I was on my knees, swishing clothes and shoes around the bathtub, it dawned on me. This was it. Eric had gotten back at me. It was over! And I didn't have a broken nose, black eye, cracked ribs, or anything.

I was so excited, I ran downstairs to tell Jerod. He was playing Nintendo with his friend Phil.

"Eric and his friends shot me with water guns full of pee!" I cried. "Isn't that *great?*"

He was really into the video game, so he just grunted.

As I went back up the steps, I heard Phil say, "Your sister is easily amused, huh?"

I wrung the water out of my clothes. I felt like I'd lost fifty pounds of fear. Eric had finally tried the first bounce.

ELEVEN

Acting like a pillow turned out to be harder than I'd expected. The whole school knew what Eric, Roger, and Lawrence had done to me, and I was getting teased all the time. Everyone thought it was hysterical. Some kids wanted to see what gross thing I'd do to Eric next, so they were egging me on, saying, "You're not going to let him make a fool of you like that, are you?" It seemed like before this all happened I had one stupid kid trying to make me mad, and now I had a whole bunch of stupid kids trying to make me mad.

"Sarah is a coward," Roger taunted me every time I saw him in the hall. I thought he was supposed to be Eric's friend, but I guess he was getting a big kick out of watching me and Eric do gross things to each other and having fun getting in on the act, and he didn't want it to end.

If there were prizes for ignoring people, I definitely would have gotten one. I just pretended they

86

were teasing somebody else named Sarah whom I'd never met.

If there were prizes for giving a cold shoulder to someone you used to hang out with all the time, then Christina deserved that one. When I was finally out of recess detention again, I cornered her just before the start of the soccer game.

"How long is it going to take before you believe me?" I demanded. "I haven't done anything to get him back, and I'm not planning anything."

Christina folded her arms over her chest. "You have been ignoring the teasing really well," she said. "But I'm still fighting with you," she added quickly.

I threw my hands up in exasperation. "You're fighting with me because I used to be fighting with Eric. That makes no sense at all!"

"It does make sense," she insisted. "Your fight with Eric made no sense—he's not your friend or your brother or cousin or anything. He's not worth fighting with."

"And your fight with me makes sense?"

Christina looked at me like the answer was so obvious a first grader would have been able to tell me. "Yes. You *are* worth fighting with. You're my best friend," she said.

I blinked at her. I'd thought I was only her *ex-*friend.

Tyrone walked up to us spinning his soccer ball on one finger. "Are you girls gonna jabber or are you gonna play?" he asked.

"Play," said Christina. As we followed him onto the field, she said to me under her breath, "Friends fight and then they *apologize* and make up." She emphasized *apologize* like it might be a new vocabulary word for me.

So now I was supposed to give up the fight with Eric, ignore all the teasing from the other kids, *and* say "I'm sorry" to Christina? I'd never in my life planned on being such a perfect child.

Fortunately the soccer game got into full swing, so I got busy running and dribbling and didn't think about the apology anymore. It was great to be out playing again. I stole the ball from Tyrone and started dribbling toward my team's goal. I was way out in front, running like a cheetah, when out of the corner of my eye I saw something coming at me from the side. I was almost to the goal, almost ready to kick the ball in, when something wide and fleshy hit me broadside and sent me tumbling onto the grass. The next thing I knew everybody was shouting.

"Get off the field!"

"She was about to score! Get out of here, you idiot!"

"Go pick on someone your own size, Bardo!"

I looked up just in time to see Eric hurrying away from the soccer field with a bunch of angry fifth graders shouting at him.

Jamal knelt down. "Are you okay?" he asked.

My ankle felt sprained, but other than that I was fine.

Jamal and Christina helped me up, and the other kids followed us to the sidelines.

"What are you going to do?" Christina asked me.

I looked right at her, stared into her eyes so maybe once and for all she'd believe me. I said it slowly and clearly. "Nothing."

"Nooooo!" Christina shook her hands like she'd touched something hot. "I think you should do something!" she cried.

My eyes bugged right out of my head. "*Now* you want me to get revenge?"

Christina shook her head. "I think you should tell a teacher. He could have really hurt you."

She had a point. My parents taught me, starting when I was little, that if somebody swipes my toy truck while we're playing in the sandbox or calls me Poo-poo Head, I don't need to tattle on them. But if the kid smacks me in the nose with the toy truck, then I'm supposed to tell anyone and everyone— parents, teacher, principal, reporter for the six o'clock news, the works.

I scratched my head. The other kids went back to the soccer game, and Christina sat down in the grass with me.

"He didn't really hurt me, though," I said. "It wasn't much worse than being slide-tackled."

She looked worried. "Maybe ignoring him isn't going to work."

I sighed. "I forgot to ask Jerod how many bounces Eric is allowed before I get to put superglue on the seat of his chair."

Christina gave me a look that was blank at first, then her eyes started to sparkle. "So it would be there waiting for him when he came back from recess?"

I nodded.

"And he wouldn't see it because it's clear?"

I nodded again.

"And he would sit on it and stick?" A smile was breaking out on her face. "And then what?"

"He wouldn't be able to get up without ripping off the seat of his pants. It would be the best view of Eric Bardo's underpants any of the sixth-grade girls have ever seen."

Christina started giggling, and a minute later both of us were lying on the grass laughing so hard we had tears on our faces.

The bell rang and it was time to go inside. I don't

know what got into me, but I grabbed Christina's hand and said, "Wait." I took a deep breath, gritted my teeth, closed my eyes, and said, "I'm sorry we missed out on doing lots of stuff together when I was in trouble."

When I opened my eyes, she was grinning. She squeezed my hand. "Okay, good," she said. "Now I'm not mad at you anymore."

We trotted toward the doors, me with a slight limp. But before we got there I stopped her again. I'd been wondering for a long time, so I had to ask. "When you went to the mall with Kelly, did you get your pictures taken at the photo booth?"

Christina laughed and put her arm around me. "Of course not," she said. "I'm saving that to do with *you.*"

TWELVE

For social studies we started a unit on Egypt. Mr. Harrison taught us all about how the Egyptians built humongous pyramids, wrapped up important dead people so they wouldn't rot, and put them inside the pyramids. Unimportant people they let rot.

Then Mr. Harrison brought out cans of paint—red, blue, yellow, white, and even gold—and told us we were going to make the best mural of Egypt ever. He unrolled a huge piece of stiff, heavy white cloth and told us we could start sketching (each work group got a square), and as soon as we were done sketching we could dig into the paints. Our group decided to do a picture of King Tutankhamen because when he died and they wrapped him up, they put a gold mask on him and surrounded him with gold jewelry. We were really excited about using the gold paint.

I thought I'd gotten rid of Eric for good, not just because I'd become so boring to tease but also because he got this stupid vest that took up all of his attention. It was this ugly pea-soup green army-looking thing with fourteen or twenty zippered pockets, and every time I walked by him anywhere he was talking about it.

"This here is the pocket where you keep all your fishhooks, and this here is the one for the bait. And look, this one is big enough so's you can stick your lunch in it, and you can fish all day without having to go back home."

At first Roger and Lawrence and the other sixth-grade boys listened to him and looked at all the pockets and tried the zippers. But when Eric kept blabbing about the same old pockets and what he was going to do with them, the older boys lost interest. Eric started showing all the fourth and fifth graders and even some third graders—anyone who would listen.

"Look, this here pocket is little, but it's just the right size for a tin full of worms. My dad says he'll come visit me next summer and take me fishing every day. That's why he sent me this vest."

The little kids mostly seemed to like playing with the zippers. I was just glad Eric was entertained and was leaving me alone.

One day I saw him trying to show the vest to Roger again. Roger stood there looking annoyed for a few minutes. Then he shoved Eric in the shoulder and demanded, "Do you really think your father is gonna come take you fishing?"

Eric lifted his chin and glared at Roger. "Yeah. Next summer."

"Has your father ever come to visit you?" Roger asked in a mean voice. "*Ever?*"

Eric glared even harder. "He's going to this time. That's why he sent me the vest."

"Would you shut up about that stupid vest?" said Roger. "We're all bored with it."

I didn't stay to watch the rest.

The next day my luck ran out. I was sitting in the lunchroom with Christina and Kelly and a bunch of other girls. All of a sudden everybody looked at something behind me and their eyes got real wide. Before I could turn around, slimy, runny ketchup rained down on my head and lap.

"Oh, no! Sarah's bleeding!" I heard Eric shout from behind me. "Go get Jamal so he can save her."

The boys at the next table laughed their heads off. Christina handed me a wad of crumpled napkins and I wiped ketchup off my cheeks. I wanted to take the wad and smash it into Eric's face.

Christina gave Eric the dirtiest look I've ever seen and yanked me away before I could deck him. "Let's go to the girls' room," she said quickly, and dragged me toward the doors.

A lunch-monitor teacher stopped us.

"Where do you girls think you're going? It's not time for recess yet," she said.

I wanted to say "Did you think I put this ketchup on this morning as part of my outfit?" but Christina answered her first.

"We're going to the girls' room to wash her off. One of the sixth-grade boys is being really mean to her."

The teacher suddenly seemed to notice that I was wearing more ketchup than most normal hamburgers. "She can go by herself," she told Christina, and made her go back to her seat.

I ran down the hall before anyone could see how stupid I looked. I didn't care if the rules said to walk—nobody else seemed to be following the rules very well.

In the restroom I held my hair under the faucet until most of the slimy ketchup was rinsed out. I tried to take deep, slow breaths so I could feel less angry, but it wasn't working.

I dried my hair with loads of brown paper towels and used them to wipe the red stuff off my jeans and shirt. I looked in the mirror. I still looked ridiculous. The ketchup had stained my shirt a disgusting orange. It looked like I'd been rolling in rotten tomatoes.

I narrowed my eyes and said into the mirror, "Eric Bardo, *you're* dead meat."

I marched down the hall to Eric's classroom. I wasn't sure what I was going to do, but it was going to be mean and it was going to make Eric sorry, and I didn't even care this time if I got caught.

I headed toward his desk. Ripping up his homework would be a good start. But as I passed the coat hooks, I saw something I'd never expected. Eric's vest was hanging there like a huge zipper-covered sock. What a find! I guessed Ms. Ortiz had finally gotten fed up with Eric's constant bragging and made him take it off.

The next thing that popped into my head was the paints we were using for our mural. I ran back to my own classroom and loaded up my backpack with several cans of paint. I could already see myself filling the zippered pockets and mumbling happily, "See, this here's the pocket for the red paint, and if you put yellow and blue in this pocket and slosh it around you get green, and this here pocket is little, but you can fit almost all of what's left of the gold paint in it . . ."

In Eric's classroom I unloaded the paint cans, laid his vest out on the floor, and unzipped all the pockets. My hands were shaking, but it was from being mad, not from being scared. If anyone came and caught me, they'd just have to wait until I was done destroying Eric's vest before they took me to the office.

I tried to open the red paint with my fingernails. The lid wouldn't budge. I reached into the small pouch of my backpack for a pen to pry it open with, and my fingers closed around the scallop shell I'd put in there. I pulled it out and turned it over in my palm. It was black with white markings. Now, I know that conch shells are supposed to remind you of the ocean if you hold them to your ear to hear the waves, and I know that scallop shells aren't supposed to remind you of the ocean like that, and I didn't even hold this one to my ear, but right then and there it reminded me of the ocean just as plain as if I were there again. It reminded me of the riptide.

I stopped working on wrecking Eric's vest and just sat there thinking. I remembered my dream and how I fought the riptide and sank down under the blue-green water. I remembered how Mr. Perez said the only way to survive a riptide is to let it carry you out all the way to its end.

Just then I heard footsteps in the hall outside. I didn't move, just waited. The footsteps came right to the classroom door.

"I thought I might find you here," Christina said. "Superglue?" she asked.

I shook my head. "Paint."

She looked down at the cans and Eric's vest on the floor, and sucked in her breath.

Before she could tell me I was going to get in trouble with Eric, Eric's teacher, *and* Mr. Harrison, I said, "But I was thinking . . . this thing with Eric is kind of like a riptide. If I go back to fighting, it's like struggling toward shore, and I'll drown or whatever—I'll be in heaps of trouble again, anyway. Kind of like drowning in detention."

Christina plopped down on the floor with me, listening.

"But if I can relax and let it carry me out to the end—I *must* be almost to the end, where Eric finally gets bored and gives up, right?"

Christina nodded.

"Then it will finally be over. And that's what I want it to be—over."

Christina fiddled with the handle on one of the paint cans. "I showed that lunch-monitor lady who Eric was and she carted him off to the office. I bet he'll be in recess detention for at least a week," she said.

"Did they sign him up for lessons in 'Appropriate Use of Ketchup' too?" I asked.

Christina laughed.

The end-of-recess bell rang and we panicked.

"Quick! We've got to get this stuff back!" I cried.

I threw Eric's vest onto its hook and we grabbed up the paint and scurried to our classroom. We shoved the paint onto its shelf just before the first kids arrived back from recess.

I knew I was giving Eric a big break, but it was worth it. I didn't want to play his game anymore. And if Roger called me a coward, I'd know he was wrong. Sometimes it takes a lot more courage *not* to fight than to fight.

THIRTEEN

Eric was in recess detention after that, but that didn't stop him from getting into more trouble. One day during lunch we heard shouting and scuffling from the other end of the lunchroom. When we stood up to see, there were Eric and Roger duking it out. Before the teachers could separate them, Eric had a bloody nose. Roger's cheek was purple the next day, and we didn't see either of them at lunch.

"Lunch detention," said Christina.

"Better him than me," I said.

If September and early October had been the "Sarah and Eric Show," late October became the "Eric and Roger Show." First Eric dumped Roger's gym shorts into the toilet in the boys' room and tried to flush them down. They didn't go, and it caused a big flood, and Ms. Ortiz made Eric help the janitor mop up all that toilet water. Then Roger swiped Eric's precious vest and wouldn't tell him where it was. Eric went whining all over the place about it, and when it turned up at the bottom of a lunchroom trash can (the lunch ladies just happened to see it through the clear plastic bag), all covered with goopy baked beans and chocolate milk, I actually saw Eric cry.

We never saw either of those guys at lunch or recess—they seemed to be on permanent detention, like I used to be.

Now I could see why kids were egging me on before—it was pretty fun to wonder what crazy thing they would do to each other next. When Roger's bike showed up after school with two stabbed tires, the next day Eric showed up with a very strange haircut (the word was, Roger had knelt on Eric's chest and hacked off his hair, saying "*This* is what scissors are for, *not* for bicycle tires!").

The best part was, Eric forgot I existed. I had refused to fight, and he'd found somebody who would, and I was off the hook.

In the meantime, I was having great fun being out of detention and living a normal kid's life. At lunch we had contests to see who could make the tallest tower of French fries. At recess Christina and I always got picked first for soccer—even before any of the boys— because we were the best players. Once, after school, Christina and I went home with Kelly on her bus. We had a great time eating microwave pizza and chasing her dog and Frisbee around the backyard.

In the middle of all this fun I actually sat down and wrote a letter to Andrea. I told her how all the kids talked with funny accents when I first got to Maryland, but that they didn't anymore. And I told her how we went to the beach in September and the water was so warm we could swim without our eyeballs freezing.

She wrote me back right away and said her mother had let her buy tall black boots with heels on them just like movie stars wear, and that she'd already gotten to use them because it had snowed two inches. I was sitting in the backyard when I read that, and I couldn't believe I'd seen the word *snow*. I was wearing shorts and a T-shirt, and my mom's pansies were still blooming. I decided that when I wrote her back I'd tell her how nice and warm it was in Maryland.

On Saturday my mom drove me and Christina to the mall. We bought plastic fangs for our Halloween costumes (both of us decided to be werewolves), rummaged through the equipment at the sports store, and ate ice cream. We ended up at the photo booth. We had to wait while these two teenage girls used it. They poofed up their hair and put on extra makeup and tried to get pictures of themselves looking gorgeous for their boyfriends.

When it was our turn, we put in our money and slipped into the booth. In the first picture we turned our lips inside out and stuck out our tongues. For the second shot I pulled my hair in front of my face so you could just see my nose, and Christina wore her plastic fangs. The third picture was a shot of the back of the photo booth, because we both leaned over to pick up Christina's fangs, which she'd dropped.

For the fourth photo we wrapped our arms around each other and laughed at how silly we were being. That's the one I hung on my bedroom wall.

Elisa Carbone lives in Maryland with her husband and her two college-age children. She spends her summers in Maine, where she visits her three nieces who, like Sarah in this book, have been known to lend hair elastics to their father on hot summer days.

A faculty member at the University of Maryland, Ms. Carbone often speaks at schools, universities, and conferences on innovative teaching methods and creative writing. She is also the author of the middle-grade novel *Corey's Story*.